Change-up

BASEBALL POEMS

by Gene Fehler
Illustrated by Donald Wu

Clarion Books • New York

Clarion Books
an imprint of Houghton Mifflin Harcourt Publishing Company
215 Park Avenue South, New York, NY 10003
Text copyright © 2009 by Gene Fehler
Illustrations copyright © 2009 by Donald Wu

Some of these poems, in a different form, appeared in *I Hit the Ball!* by Gene Fehler,
published by McFarland & Company in 1996 and now out of print.

The illustrations were executed in acrylic and colored pencil.
The text was set in 12-point Boton.

For information about permission to reproduce selections from this book,
write to Permissions, Houghton Mifflin Harcourt Publishing Company,
215 Park Avenue South, New York, NY 10003.

www.clarionbooks.com

Manufactured in China.

Library of Congress Cataloging-in-Publication Data
Fehler, Gene, 1940–
Change-up : baseball poems / by Gene Fehler ; illustrated by Donald Wu.
p. cm.
ISBN 978-0-618-71962-4
1. Baseball—Juvenile poetry. 2. Children's poetry, American. I. Wu, Donald, ill. II. Title.
PS3556.E37C47 2008
811'.54—dc22   2008021950

WKT 10 9 8 7 6 5 4 3 2 1

For Mireille Elise, Gabrielle Lisette,
and Kaya Dawn
—G.F.

For Dugald
—D.W.

Snow Baseball

Six of us stomp onto the February field
through the snow blanket that covers it
like a cold, crisp cotton tarp,
snow soft enough for sliding
beneath the fluff of flung snowballs
from woolly-hatted third basemen,
their tosses to first base
only weak winter imitations
of summer's bullet throws.

I step up to the plate, hurl
a dazzling fly snowball toward short,
and plow through snow, slipping and sloshing.
As my snowball shatters
against the shortstop's mittened hands,
I dive headfirst across where I guess
first base must be, my face skidding
through sparkling snowdust.

I bounce up,
warmed by the kind of thoughts
that help get me through February,
the hardest month.

Fielder's Mitt

On the shelf my mitt,
stiff from winter's bench-
warming cold,
waits for spring,
for mud-scuffed balls
slapping past, taunting
"Catch me if you can!"
—a challenge
that thaws my mitt
for a chase
through any mud-warmed
ballpark
in suddenly spring.

First Practice

After a winter of waiting, it's finally time.
Sammy and I outrace everyone to Coach's car.
Coach opens the trunk, and I see junk:
golf clubs,
a tire jack,
a pencil,
a dirty towel,
a pair of golf shoes.

I also see great stuff:
a green canvas bat bag
and, tangled amid jumper cables,
a greenish brown baseball,
its scuffed cover seeming to smile
as it starts to roll
toward Sammy and me.

Gramps

Gramps pitched in the minor leagues,
tells me stories that give me hope
I can make it myself someday.

Sometimes he throws to me in the backyard,
spits into the worn pocket of his tattered mitt,
barely larger than his hand.

He rubs the ball around,
tells me before each pitch
to hold my glove still.

If he ever throws it straight,
I will.

Gramps's Tough Pitches

1. Knuckleball

It floats.

It dips like a pirate ship
riding on waves that toss it
up
and
down.

Bat in hand,
I wait and wait
and here it comes,
pulled by strings
this way
and that—

where's it at?

I wait and wait.
It nears the plate

and now
and now

my bat swings
under (maybe over)
it

too soon.
Or was the swing

too late?

2. Fastball

The fastball
comes.
I swing.
I blink.

It goes
right through
my bat,
I think.

3. Slow Curve

Curving like a half moon,
it sweeps toward me.

My body leans back;
the ball blends and teases.

It misses my bat
whenever it pleases.

Window Noises

I really hate
    to hear the sound
    of windows when
I'm playing ball.

I've noticed that
    unless it breaks,
    a window makes
no sound at all.

Perspective

When I'm

in the field,

the open spaces

are as big

as the Sahara,

with room enough

for a thousand

humpbacked

camels.

When I'm in the batter's
box, a thousand fielders
stand shoulder-to-shoulder
with fielder's mitts big
as bushel baskets in a
space way smaller than
my tiny bedroom closet,
all ready to snag every one
of my blistering line drives.

Bat Poem

I wrote a poem with my baseball bat.
It was only four lines long
and it didn't even rhyme,
but it was a great poem.

The first line was "Touched first base."
Line two was "Touched second base."
The third line was "Touched third base."
The last line was "Touched home plate."
The title that my bat gave the poem
was HOME RUN.

It was the best poem my bat and I ever wrote.

First Loss

I dropped the ball
and the sky fell; scared
little kids at horror movies
could not have sent screams
cutting so loud my way as those
coming from the splintered bleachers.

I dropped the ball
into the infield dust,
where it will blow
around in the attic
of my memory, mixing with
cries of disappointed parents.

Through long winter months
of imagining a summer full
of heroic moments,
of game-winning hits and catches,
not once,
not once
did I drop the ball.

Baseball Dream 1

My baseball dream
turns into a nightmare.
My mitt becomes a trampoline,
sending each ball I try to catch
high into the sky.

With each *SPRONG*
I think the ball will go into orbit
while runners dressed
in red clown suits
with purple shoes
and fluffy blue and orange hair
circle the bases.

I finally toss the mitt away
and try to catch the ball with my bare hands.

But right in the middle
of a new, pleasant dream
a lazy fly ball floats
                down
                down

                        higher
                    higher
                higher
and then bounces high

after it hits
my
trampoline
hands.

Dad Alert

Dad hits pop-ups
so high that airplanes
make U-turns in the sky
and birds dive for cover
whenever they see
Dad in the backyard
on a summer evening
with a baseball bat
in his hands,
a Chicago Cubs cap
on his head,
and a wide grin
on his face.

Mom

Some moms come late from work,
make you eat broccoli, yell because
you tracked mud on the carpet.

Some moms are too busy
to ever come to your ballgames
or even ask if you won or lost.

My mom pitches me batting practice,
hits me grounders, then dives
in the dirt to field mine. At breakfast

some moms nag about homework or how
you're dressed for school. Mine grabs
the morning paper to read the box scores.

Pitching Music

I find my rhythm,
swinging my arm
to the beat
of a sweet song.

The ball
starts its lullaby
in my pitching
hand,

sings
all the way
into the
muffled darkness

of
my catcher's
pillowed
mitt.

My Best Hitting

I step to the plate,
ready to play a medley
of my favorite summer
music.

My fingers drum
the bat handle,
limber up,
play the scales,
perform
their own sweet
melodies:

a banjo bunt,
a saxophone single,
a trumpeting triple,
a harp-sweet,
horn-blowing homer,

and with each at-bat
the fans
behind the rusted screen
back of home plate
like concert-goers
roar,
stand,
and demand
an encore.

Surprise Two-Strike Bunt

With a runner perched on third,
the other team's worst hitter
slides his hand up the bat handle,
lays down a bunt—
almost perfect.

It bounces,
skids,
wavers,
slides,
bounces on the foul line
like a tightrope walker.

Too late to make the play,
I stand frozen
near my third baseman.

We watch as the ball
clings to chalked edges;
and,
as it inches
up the line
and teases us,
taunts us,
stretches
toward third base's shadow,
all we can do
is hold our breath

and hope.

Change-up

I wind up, kick high, throw the 3-2 pitch.

My catcher, "Automatic Out" Albert,
watches it float toward him,

sets his catcher's mitt on the ground,
slides a *Baseball Digest* from his back pocket,

and reads an article, probably about
some sore-armed has-been pitcher.

The ump pulls a harmonica from under his hat
and plays a verse of "You're a Slowpoke."

The batter falls asleep waiting for the ball to arrive.

When it finally does, there's nothing
for Albert to do except close his magazine,
pick up his mitt, and hold it open for the ball.

There's nothing for the batter to do
except dream of how he might have clobbered
that pitch, had he only stayed awake.

There's nothing for the ump to do
but pause in the middle of the final chorus
to shout "Strike three!"

And there's nothing for me to do
except look in toward Albert
and grin.

Ted

Ted's really cool. He's lots of fun.
  But he can't field or hit or run.
He tries real hard, but still the guy
  gets more bench time than anyone.

He hardly ever gets to play,
  yet comes to practice every day.
Our whole team cheers him on, but luck
  just never seems to come his way

The uniform Ted got? It's small;
  he hardly fits in it at all.
His pants? They split when he bent down
  to try to catch a hard ground ball.

And in the wash, the "T" (in red)
  came off—it changed his name to Ed.
But he just shrugged and grinned. "At least
  I *have* a uniform," he said.

Gehrig

Sammy's dog, Gehrig, just a mutt,
spends most innings chasing squirrels
or chewing on bones.

Except when Sammy steps to the plate.

Gehrig stops in the middle
of the chase or drops the bone in mid-chew
and stiffens up, tail quivering.
He barks one time.
Then he pauses in reverent silence
and watches Sammy
while Sammy stares down the pitcher.

Once the at-bat is over, Gehrig barks again—
twice if Sammy gets on base,
once if he doesn't.
Then he returns to his squirrels or his bone
or stretches out in the shade of the big oak
just within range of a medium foul ball
off the right field line.

I've never seen any dog in our town—
with or without fancy papers—
show its owner the attention
that Sammy gets from Gehrig
whenever Sammy steps
into the batter's box.

At game's end,
as we walk from the ballfield together,
Gehrig right beside us,
and Sammy does a play-by-play of the game,
you can see the mutt's ears perk up
when Sammy tells the good parts.

Superstitions

Sammy chews fresh bubble gum
  in every other inning.
Larry wears long underwear
  as long as we keep winning.

Before each time at bat, Miguel
  rubs dirt on both his knees.
Coach says a prayer each time Ted hits—
  looks skyward and begs, "Please."

Bobby turns a somersault
  each inning at first base.
Before each curve that Gabby throws
  she makes a funny face.

Well, I'm not superstitious.
  Not me. No, not a bit.
But now I'd better kiss my bat:
  it's almost time to hit.

Dusk

A favorite time

is twilight,
when some of us from my team
get together to hit
fly balls to each other
in old man Parker's vacant lot,
bats blazing in the setting sun,
the thump of horsehide
and flashing leather;

then, as the ball,
almost hidden
in the gray of dusk,
falls into my waiting glove,

I hear the perfectly timed
sweet sound
of Mom's call
from down the street:
"Come on home."

Bedtime

Sometimes I lie awake
and count base hits
the way some people count sheep:

1 – a bunt down the third-base line
2 – a squibbler toward first
3 – a line drive to center
4 – a bloop double over second
5 – a long double in the gap
6 – a triple high off the fence
7 – a home run that never comes down

and when I'm due to pitch the next day,
I pray I'll fall asleep before I count
all the way to
10.

The Umpire

That blind old ump behind the plate
    is such a gruesome sight!
His eyes are like tomatoes;
    his teeth are long and white.

Hot steam and crackling flames shoot out
    from both his ears and nose,
and he calls "Strike" on everything
    the other pitcher throws,

especially when I'm at bat.
    And oh, it makes me mad!
But when he doesn't ump my games,
    I really love my dad.

Baseball Dream 2

The most amazing play I've seen
  happened just last night.
A fly ball high into the sky
  struck and broke a light.

Some jagged glass cut through the ball
  and sliced it right in two.
The center fielder found both halves,
  picked them up, and threw.

The fans let out the biggest roar
  I think I've ever heard:
The pieces threw two runners out—
  at second and at third.

I Visualized the Ball

I visualized the ball so well
I could see every stitch
from the moment it left
the pitcher's long skinny fingers
and rotated toward me,
spinning faster than the earth itself.

I visualized the ball so well
I could read every word written on it.
The name on the baseball, Spalding,
spoke to me, saying, "How do you do?"
"Fine," I said, and I hit the ball
smack on that name and visualized it
all the way over the fence.

The only thing is, the next time
the pitcher threw me that same pitch,
I forgot to visualize
where it was supposed to go,
and the catcher visualized it
right into
his big mitt.

Gabby

She wears her cap pulled down,
shading her face and covering
her long hair.
Sometimes the other team
thinks Gabby's a boy,
but that doesn't concern her.
Or us, either.

It's her pitching that matters,
the slow curves that keep
the big Carleyville sluggers off balance,
setting them up for her hard fastballs.

From shortstop I cheer her on,
then help her out of a jam
in the last inning by starting
a game-ending double play,
a play so nice she gives me
a quick hug—
and I'm not even embarrassed
that someone might see.

Bench View

The game looks different
from the dugout,
where I'm taking my turn
as a bench-warmer.

The game unfolds before me
in greens and browns
of grass and ground,
blue and white
of sky and cloud,

and in between:
running bodies,
shouting bodies,
and Ted, a smiling body,
playing the last inning
in the outfield.

I see the breeze-tossed,
sun–soaked ball
dancing,
drifting
with a mind of its own,
fighting the sun and wind,

darting
toward Ted,
who staggers,
almost skips
as if the ground burns his feet,
before he snags it
inches from the ground
and, grinning,
turns toward our dugout
and bows.

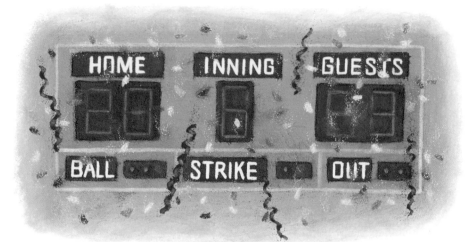

The Other Team

I don't like the other team,
    although Dad thinks I should.
But I don't like the Tigers.
    Those guys are just too good.

I wish, instead, they couldn't hit
    or catch or throw or run.
I wish that we could slaughter them.
    Oh, boy! Would that be fun!

But Dad and Coach just don't agree.
    They want a thrilling game,
the kind you get when everyone
    plays pretty much the same.

They say it's more exciting when
    the outcome is in doubt
until the very final pitch,
    until the final out.

That might be so, but still I think
    that I would rather see
a game where we score twenty runs
    and they score, maybe, three.

When Dad Is Away

Dad taught me how
to hold my bat
away from my body
when I swing
and how to let the ball
spin off my fingertips
when I throw
and how to oil my glove
and wrap string around it
with a ball inside
so when I sleep
the pocket will remember
the ball just as clearly
as I remember
my dad's face.

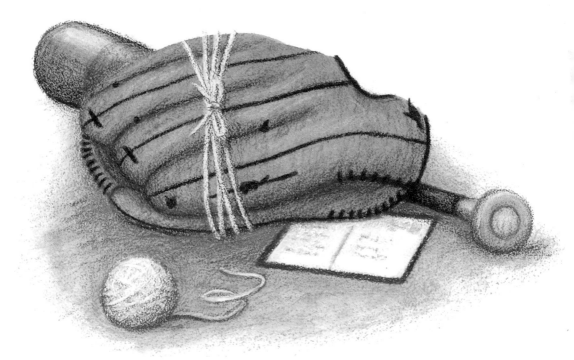

Cucumber

The day before our game against the Tigers,
Sammy and I practiced in his yard.
The cucumber patch watched us,
yawned under the August sun,
swallowed my only baseball.

We stomped in,
ripped at its throat,
plowed through its perfect camouflage,
searched in vain
for my brown-green precious ball.

"My cucumber patch!" Sammy's mother shrieked.
She flew through the back door,
her eyes full of fire.
Sammy picked the ball up,
but I had already started running.
I was halfway down the alley toward home
when the ball thudded behind me.

It rolled, cool as a cucumber, to my feet.
I glanced back, saw his mother grab
Sammy by the shoulders and shake him.

I joked about it later with "Automatic Out" Albert,
who caught Sammy's fireball pitches
for six innings the next day,
chattering all the while,
"Fire the old cucumber in, Sammy!"

Even though he shut them out,
I didn't see Sammy smile even once.

Sad Summer Days

On the dugout
roof
raindrops thud
and laugh—
they're mocking me

    as
        infield
            rivers
                wash
                    my
                        baseball
                            dreams
                                far out
                                  to sea.

"Automatic Out" Albert

Albert, our catcher, big as a barn,
can catch any pitch our pitchers throw,
can block any ball in the dirt.

We cheer his catching
but groan whenever he bats.
He closes his eyes when he swings.
Swish. Swish. Swish.
Albert, the automatic out.

Down a run in the last inning with two outs,
we sit gloomily on our bench,
knowing all too well how the game will end
with "Automatic Out" Albert at bat:
Swish. Swish. Swish.
A bitter defeat.

Instead, we rise as one
at an unexpected sound:
a mighty *CLANK!*

Albert takes forever rounding the bases.
Our bench sags in the middle
when he plops down,
tired from his home-run jog,
or else from the minutes
of back-slapping celebration
after he crossed the plate.

A big smile stays on Albert's face
long after the game is over.
It's almost as if he knows
that after his game-winning home run
he's lost his nickname
forever.

Our Last Game

Visions of base hits
and diving catches
and cheering teammates
and green summer grasses
flash through my mind
while Sammy and I watch
Coach yank the bases out
like decayed teeth.

The infield gums its goodbye.

Toothless now
until its dentist appointment
in the spring,
all it can eat
during the next long months
is the soft snow
of winter.

In December

Our ballfield is barren now,
except for snow,
except for seeds of memories
of all of us who played here,
memories planted deep,
seeds that years from now—
when we are grown
and many miles away
and the field is parking lot
or apartment buildings—
will grow into feats
larger than all the hits
we never got,
all the plays we never made.

Ballfield in February

Home plate shivers
in its sleep
under ten inches of snow.

It dreams of batters scared,
runs scored.

It waits for melting moments,
for seasons of sunshine,
for booming bats,
for the whispering *whoosh*
of the ump's broom.

Home plate
will awaken fast enough
when spring comes.